## Chapter One

Josh was on his way home from
school when he saw the sign.

It said:

Josh stopped and blinked. Then he
read the sign very slowly, twice over,
to see that he had got it right.
The sign was on the old tree at the

end of Cowper's Lane. The sign hadn't been there in the morning when Josh went by on his way to school, and it was only just there now.

It came, and it went, flickeringly. Sometimes it was there, and sometimes it wasn't, all in the same split second.

"Look at that!" he said to Marge.

"What?" said Marge.

"*That*," said Josh, pointing at the sign, which was there when he pointed, but *wasn't* when Marge looked.

"I don't see anything, Josh," said Marge. "Come on, we'll be late for tea."

"But . . ." said Josh.

"I'm not hanging about playing games, little Josh!" said Marge, and she marched on, leaving her brother behind her.

3

"WAIT!" Josh shouted.

"No," said Marge, over her shoulder.

"But . . . but . . . there's a sign on the tree."

"No, there isn't," said Marge. "I've looked, and I *know* there isn't. You're bonkers, Josh!"

And she went off, leaving Josh standing in front of the sign.

He read it again, carefully.

SMALL GHOST SEEKS
CUMFY HAUNT
NO GOLDFISH
APPLY WITHOUT

*It should be 'apply within'*, Josh thought, because he had seen signs

like that before in Mr Shardi's shop
. . . although the signs in Mr
Shardi's shop didn't *come* and *go*, the
way the one on the tree did. Still . . .

"Without *what?*" muttered Josh.

"Goldfish," said the Ghost.

Josh *heard* the word 'goldfish', but
he couldn't *see* anyone.

"Who said that?" he demanded.

"I did," said the Ghost.

This time, Josh was sure no one was there.

"A g-g-g-g-g-host!" Josh stuttered.

"But only a small one," said the Ghost. "I'd fit in almost anywhere."

"But . . . but . . ." Josh was scared and interested, all at the same time. He had never met a ghost before, and he wasn't quite certain that he had met one this time, because he couldn't see the ghost. He could only hear it.

"Is that your schoolbag?" asked the Ghost.

"Y-e-s," said Josh uncertainly.

Suddenly his schoolbag gave a wriggle, and a lurch, and banged against his back.

"Right, I'm in," said the Ghost in

a muffled voice from inside the
schoolbag. "Very satisfactory, apart
from all the crumbs and sweetie
papers!"

"I . . . I . . . I . . ." said Josh,
grabbing his schoolbag, which gave a
sort of wriggle.

"*Careful*," said the Ghost.

"Sorry," said Josh.

"It's time we were going home for
tea," said the Ghost. "Mustn't be
late, or your mum will be cross."

7

"J-O-S-H!" Marge yelled, coming back down the lane. "Do hurry up!"

"I told you!" said a muffled voice from the schoolbag.

"Mum's going to skin you alive for mucking about, little Josh," said Marge, and she grabbed Josh and marched him off down the lane.

*Bang* went the schoolbag on Josh's back.

"Oh!" and "Ouch!" and "Would you believe it!" went the Ghost in the bag, but Marge didn't hear it.

Josh did, but he didn't say anything, because he didn't know what to say.

## Chapter Two

"Four places," said Mum, looking at the knives and forks. "And there are only *three* of us. Who laid the table?"

"I didn't!" said Josh.

"I didn't!" said Marge.

"I *did*," said the Ghost, but nobody heard it except Josh.

"You can't count!" said Josh.

"Who can't count?" said Mum.

"Whoever laid this table can't count!" said Marge. "And it wasn't *me*!"

"I *can* count," said the Ghost,

sounding hurt. "One for you, Josh,
one for Marge, one for your mum,
and one for me."

"They don't know you're here,"
said Josh.

"Who doesn't know who is here?"
said Mum.

"Er . . . nobody," said Josh,
getting confused.

"That's right," said the Ghost
cheerfully. "No Body!"

It was meant to be a joke, but Josh
didn't laugh, because he was
beginning to realise that the Ghost
was a problem.

Mum sat down, and Josh sat
down, and the Ghost sat down, and
Marge sat down on the Ghost.

"Ouch!" went Marge, in the
middle of sitting *down*, and she shot
*up* again suddenly, and almost
knocked the table over.

"Marge!' said Mum.

"Somebody pinched my bottom!" said Marge, going red.

"Sit down at once and don't tell lies, Marge," said Mum. "Nobody pinched your bottom. There's nobody there."

"*Exactly*," said the Ghost, floating round to the seat next to Josh, and getting ready to tuck in.

For a small Ghost with no body, it tucked in rather a lot.

"I've never seen you two eat such a tea!" said Mum, when they'd finished. "All that food! I can't think where you put it."

"Neither can I," said Josh.

"Ahem!" coughed the Ghost politely.

After tea, Josh and Mum did the dishes and Marge walked the dog.

The ghost went with her. The dog always enjoyed a walk after tea, but this time it didn't.

It kept sniffing and snuffling around, and annoying Marge, who couldn't see what it was sniffing and snuffling at.

The dog (which was called 'Dog') had a very worried walk, and came back home still snuffling, although it stopped when the Ghost slipped off into Josh's schoolbag.

Josh began to think that the Ghost had gone, as mysteriously as it had come . . . or maybe he'd imagined it all.

But he was wrong.

The Ghost was busy, inside the schoolbag, getting organised.

First it threw out all the old sweetie papers and crumbs, which it neatly parcelled up in a page from Josh's jotter, and put in the bin.

The Ghost wrote out two signs, very carefully. One said, 'Private – Keep Out' and the other said,

'Resting – Do Not Disturb'. The Ghost stuck them on the schoolbag, one above the other.

Then it made a sleeping bag from Josh's pencil case and climbed in and went to sleep, because it had had a busy day house-hunting.

## Chapter Three

It was midnight when Josh woke up.

He didn't usually wake up at midnight. He was usually fast asleep until getting-up time, but *something* wakened him.

It was a sound.

A very small sound

*Tinkle*
*Tinkle*
*Tinkle*

coming from the hall.

Burglars, thought Josh, and he wondered what to do. Then . . .

Tinkle Tinkle Tinkle

and

Tinkle
Tinkle
Tinkle

SPLOSH!

came from the kitchen and somebody yelled

oooo O A A A H !

in a very small voice which made Josh realise that it wasn't burglars at all. It was the Ghost.

*I'd better go and see what has happened to it*, thought Josh, and he climbed out of bed, and padded into the kitchen.

The Ghost was standing next to Dog's dish, dripping onto the tiles.

"Who put that dish there?" it said angrily.

"Mum did," said Josh. "She always puts water out for Dog at night."

"Nobody told me!" grumbled the Ghost, but it wasn't making a joke about No Body, because it was all wet, and cold, and shivery after falling into Dog's dish, and it wasn't in a jokey mood.

Josh couldn't see it, but he could see the drips.

"So much for *clanking*!" said the Ghost.

"Clanking?" said Josh.

"Clanking," said the Ghost firmly. "That's what ghosts do. Clank-clank-clank, like this."

And it went

round Dog's dish.

"That sounds like a tinkle to me," said Josh reasonably, because it did.

"It may sound like a tinkle to you, but it is a clank," said the Ghost. "I'm rather proud of my clanks, considering I can only manage a very small chain."

Josh thought for a bit. "Why can you only manage a very small chain?" he said.

"Because I'm only a very small ghost," said the Ghost, and it tinkled softly off to the bathroom, to dry itself on a towel.

"JOSH?" said Mum. "Josh, what are you doing up at this hour?"

"Er . . . nothing," said Josh. "I just woke up."

"Back to bed, N-O-W," said Mum.

"I'm going to have trouble with this Ghost," Josh muttered and he went back to bed.

## Chapter Four

There was no sign of the Ghost in the morning, but Josh knew it was still there, because he could see the

Resting – Do Not Disturb

sign flickering beneath the

Private – Keep Out

sign on his schoolbag in the hall.

The Ghost was recovering from the effects of its dip in Dog's dish.

It didn't show up until mid-morning and when it did show up it *didn't*, because of course nobody could see it, because it was that sort of ghost. Josh knew that it was there when it sat down in front of the television and asked, "Anything good on?"

"There's a programme about sharks," said Josh.

"Sharks?" said the Ghost. "I don't like programmes about sharks."

"Why not?" said Josh.

"I was swallowed by a goldfish once," said the Ghost.

"What's that got to do with sharks? Sharks are nothing like goldfish," said Josh.

"They are from the inside," said the Ghost with a shudder.

Josh switched off the TV.

"About this Haunt," said the Ghost.

"What Haunt?" said Josh.

"The Haunt I'm here to do," said the Ghost. "In return for board and lodging in your schoolbag. Haunting

is what ghosts are *for*, you know.
Now, what sort of Haunt had you in
mind?"

"Er . . . what sorts are there?"
asked Josh, because he wasn't sure if
he wanted to be haunted at all.

"Well, there's clanking of course,"
said the Ghost, and it paused
hopefully. "I'm rather good at
clanking. I usually clank but . . ."

"No clanking," said Josh.

"I can move things about," said
the Ghost. "That can be very scary,"
and it picked up the flower vase and
floated it round the room.

"Put it down!" yelled Josh,
because his mum was very particular
about her flower vase.

"I take it that moving things is

*out*," said the Ghost. "In that case I could *moan*."

"I don't think your moaning would be any better than your clanking," said Josh. "That is, I don't think Mum would like it. Clanking, that is, or moaning, or flower vase moving . . ."

"How about rattling bones?" said the Ghost.

"Have you got any?" said Josh.

"I could get some," said the Ghost.

"I don't think Mum would like rattling bones," said Josh. "I don't think Mum would really like being haunted at all."

There was a long silence, followed by a sad sniff.

"In that case, I'd better go," said the Ghost.

"But . . . but . . ."

"I can't stay where I'm not wanted," said the Ghost, its voice floating back toward Josh as it went out through the door.

"Ghost! Ghost! Hold on a minute, I've got an idea!" shouted Josh.

But the Ghost was . . .

. . . GONE.

## Chapter Five

"Josh has gone mad, Mum," said Marge.

"What?" said Mum.

"He keeps talking to his schoolbag," said Marge.

"Don't be silly, Marge," said Mum.

"I'm not," said Marge. "Josh is. Imagine talking to a schoolbag."

Marge went out to the front of the house.

Five minutes later Marge came back.

"Mum," she said. "Josh is walking up and down the lane with an old chain, clanking it."

"I expect he is pretending he's a train," said Mum.

"I *expect* he's bonkers," said Marge.

But Josh wasn't bonkers. He was Ghost-hunting. He wasn't sure how to Ghost-hunt, and the only thing he could think of was to clank up and down the lane, and hope the Ghost would hear him.

He did a lot of clanking, but the Ghost didn't turn up. Josh felt very lonely without his Ghost.

"Mum!" said Marge.

"Yes, Marge?"

"Josh has started talking to trees," said Marge, standing at the gate, and looking down the lane at Josh.

Mum didn't say anything: she was fed up with Marge's stories, but not as fed up as Josh was, talking to a Ghost he was sure was there, and getting no answer.

Then . . .

"I'm getting cross, Ghost!" he shouted at the tree. "I know you're there . . . aren't you?"

"No," said a voice.

"It's you! It's you! I knew you were there."

"It isn't me," said the Ghost, very cunningly. "It isn't me. It is just Another Ghost that sounds like me."

"I see," said Josh, considering it.

"This Other Ghost has come back to tell you that I won't be haunting you anymore, because there's no proper haunting work to do at your house," said the Ghost. "No clanking, no vase lifting, no bone rattling, no moaning, no nothing."

"But there is *something*," Josh said slowly. "If you were here I could tell you all about it."

There was a long silence, and then the Ghost, remembering how comfortable Josh's schoolbag had been, and how warm and cosy it had felt in the pencil case sleeping bag, said carefully, "Tell the Other Ghost about it, and the Other Ghost can tell me."

"I've . . . er . . . thought up a Haunt, Other Ghost," said Josh.

"What sort?" said the voice.

"Er . . . *helpful* haunting. That's it!" said Josh.

"Hmmm," said the Ghost.

"You could . . . you could help me with my homework," said Josh. "And you could do things round the house."

"What things?" said the Ghost. "Clanking?"

"A little clanking, when there's nobody there but you and me," said Josh. "And . . . and . . . you could walk Dog."

"Ghosts don't walk dogs," said the Ghost grandly.

"All right, no dog walking," said Josh.

"Ghosts have their pride, you
know," said the Ghost, sniffily.
"Ghosts don't go back to houses
where they are not needed."

"But you *are* needed," Josh burst
out. "*I need you*. I need you so that I'll
have someone to play with who isn't
rotten Marge. Please, Ghost?"

There was a pause, while the Ghost thought about it.

"It is the *Other* Ghost you're talking to," said the Ghost carefully.

"Get the *Other* Ghost to tell you all about it," said Josh.

"I'll go and see if I can find me," said the Ghost.

Josh put his schoolbag on the ground, with the top flap open.

He waited and waited and waited and . . .

. . . *flap* went the schoolbag
and . . .

"Right, I'm in!" said the Ghost.

They went back to Josh's house
and Josh hung the schoolbag up in
the hall.

The Ghost got busy.

It wrote:

Private – Keep Out

on a sign which it stuck on top of the
schoolbag and then it wrote:

Resting – Do Not Disturb

on a sign which it stuck just below
the Private – Keep Out sign.

And then it hopped back into its
pencil case sleeping bag . . .

. . . and then it had another idea.
It hopped out of the sleeping bag and
wrote another sign

which it stuck right on the front of
the schoolbag.

"Dunroamin?" said Josh. "What
does that mean?"

"It's short for DONE
ROAMING," the Ghost said. "It's
the name I'm calling my house. It
means I'm staying here forever!"

And the Ghost did.